ROBOT RUNAWAY

TONY BRADMAN   JAKE HILL

LONDON·SYDNEY

Franklin Watts
First published in Great Britain in 2019 by The Watts Publishing Group

Series Editor: Adrian Cole
Project Editor: Katie Woolley
Designer: Cathryn Gilbert
Illustrations: Jake Hill

HB ISBN 978 1 4451 5592 0
PB ISBN 978 1 4451 5593 7
Library ebook ISBN 978 1 4451 6360 4

Printed in China

MIX
Paper from
responsible sources
FSC® C104740

Franklin Watts
An imprint of
Hachette Children's Group
Part of The Watts Publishing Group
Carmelite House
50 Victoria Embankment
London EC4Y 0DZ

An Hachette UK Company
www.hachette.co.uk

www.franklinwatts.co.uk

Layla   Jayden   Caleb

They are…

"That did not go to plan," said Layla.

"I can't control the robot. It has run away. We must get it back," said the professor.

"Prof, is it dangerous?" asked Jayden.

"Er...yes," replied the professor.

"Let's go!" said Caleb.

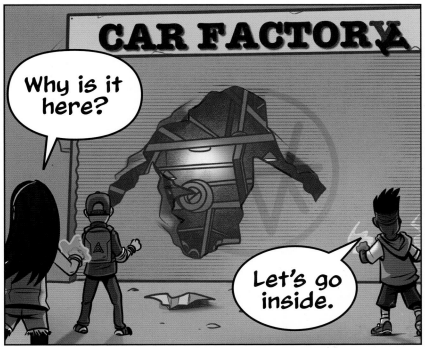

13

"But now the bits are small robots," said Jayden.

"Hey! They are getting bigger!" said Layla.

"I'll call the prof," said Caleb.

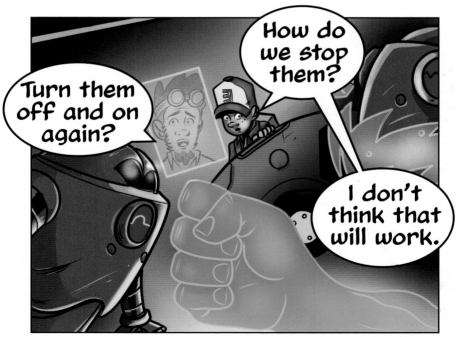

21

"I'll link to the robots," said Caleb.

"Here they come..." said Jayden.